THE GREENHOUSE KIDS
DAN DELION'S SECRET

Canadä

*The Publishers acknowledge the financial assistance of the
Government of Canada through the Book Publishing Industry
Development Program (BPIDP) for our publishing activities.*

Library and Archives Canada Cataloguing in Publication

Awad, Shelley, 1958-
  The greenhouse kids : Dan Delion's secret / Shelley
Awad ; illustrations by Constance Rose Zonta.

For ages 8-12.
ISBN 978-0-88887-379-8

  I. Zonta, Constance Rose II. Title. III. Title: Dan Delion's
secret.

PS8601.W335G74 2009   jC813'.6   C2009-902468-3

Illustrations and cover design by Constance Rose Zonta
Printed and bound in Canada on acid free paper.

THE GREENHOUSE KIDS
DAN DELION'S SECRET

BY SHELLEY AWAD

Borealis Press
Ottawa, Canada
2009

For my son, Aaron. I'll always remember our library nights.

Acknowledgements

I would like to thank

My husband, Mitch, for your wonderful ideas, for your words of encouragement, and for believing in me.

Constance for your patience, hard work and dedication.

Marty for generously donating your valuable time and advice.

Janine for your suggestions.

Borealis Press for making this book possible. Special thanks to Frank and Janet.

My mother, Glenna, for raising me as a reader, and my father, Abbey, who raised me as a gardener.

Contents

List of Illustrations

CHAPTER 1
WHO TO TELL

Dan Delion rarely slept in on a Saturday. The early morning sunlight streamed through his bedroom window, coaxing him awake. He rubbed the sleep out of his eyes and stretched his long skinny arms toward the ceiling before bolting out of bed.

It was the last day of May, and it was a perfect day for his favourite hobby, hunting bugs. He jumped into a pair of brown shorts that he grabbed off the floor, and pulled a bright yellow tee shirt over his head. Dan combed his thick spiky blonde hair and dashed downstairs to the kitchen to eat a bowl of cereal. After gulping down his second glass of milk, he pulled on his white socks, tied his high-top running shoes, and ran out the front door, letting it slam shut behind him.

1

Seedington was a small town in northern Ontario with winding country roads that were lined with thick pine trees. All was quiet, except for the sounds of birds chirping and Dan's running shoes crunching as they hit the gravel road. Once he reached the outskirts of town, he began jogging up a hill toward an abandoned old mansion that was covered with vines of ivy. A cemetery was located in the front yard, and its three tombstones made the mansion especially spooky. Years ago, both the front and back yards boasted beautiful gardens. Over time, the empty mansion became run-down and the grounds were filled with weeds, tall grasses and large overgrown plants and shrubs. Dan thought that this made the mansion grounds an ideal place to hunt for bugs.

It was rumoured that the old mansion was haunted, but Dan, who didn't believe in ghosts, wasn't scared one little bit. He ran up the hill, excited about what new bugs he might discover. He reached down and checked his right pocket, making double sure that he had

2

his magnifying glass. He seldom left home without it, and, as he soon found out, it was a very good thing that he had it with him today.

Shortly after Dan arrived at the mansion, he stumbled upon the biggest secret of his life. In fact, it was probably the biggest secret in the entire town of Seedington. Maybe even all of Ontario! Dan shook his head in disbelief, and he pinched himself more than once. He tried to run home fast, but his long skinny legs felt like jelly. He finally reached the bottom of the hill, out of breath, and checked his watch. He was surprised to see that it was almost noon. Dan closed his big brown eyes for a moment, trying to remember everything that had happened to him at the mansion. He wasn't sure which one of his three best friends he should tell his secret to first.

Should it be Holly Hocks, who lived next door to him? Or perhaps Foxy Gloves, who was one of his classmates. Or, would it be his very best friend since kindergarten, Johnny Jump-Ups? Dan was both afraid and excited as he ran his hands through his spiky hair, trying

to figure out who would be easiest to find.

Holly Hocks, who was a year older than Dan, loved to shop. She spent every Saturday at the Seedington Mall. Holly was very tall and pretty, and she and Dan had been neighbours their entire lives. Her long thick chestnut hair was parted in the middle, and quite often she tucked it behind her ears. She had a tiny face with rosy pink cheeks and big blue eyes, and she always dressed in the coolest clothes, usually pink from head to toe. Dan did not want to waste time searching through the mall, so he decided against finding Holly.

Johnny Jump-Ups might not be easy to find either. He was always hungry and he loved food. Since it was almost lunchtime, Johnny might be at home, or in any of the town's many restaurants. Johnny's short hair was so dark that it looked purple. Oddly, he had one streak of bright yellow hair that hung over one ear. His eyebrows looked as purple as his hair, and they arched overtop of his small brown eyes. He had a small nose, and huge dimples appeared whenever he smiled. He was the

4

shortest boy in his class and he was also quite plump. Johnny loved to tell jokes, and he was very charming and friendly.

Suddenly, it dawned on Dan that he was sure to find Foxy Gloves. On a warm, sunny day like today, she'd be selling lemonade from the stand her father built in front of her house on Cedar Street. He smiled as he pictured Foxy, who loved to dress up in her mother's old clothes. She also liked to dress her cute, scruffy-faced dog Madison. Foxy, who was very small, always wore a pair of her mother's long white gloves. She was nearly a full foot shorter than Dan and Holly, who were the two tallest kids in the entire school. Her shiny red curls bounced up and down when she walked, and her fiery green eyes were very bright. Freckles dotted her creamy white skin, especially on top of her small nose. Everyone adored Foxy and Madison, especially Holly, who had been her very best friend for as long as Dan could remember. Foxy Gloves would be the easiest to find, Dan thought.

He started running to Foxy's lemonade stand.

CHAPTER 2
CRASH

The lemonade stand was only a few blocks away, near the corner of Cedar and Maple streets. Just as Dan turned the corner onto Cedar Street, he ran smack into Jason Seedy, the class bully, who was nicknamed Speedy Seedy because he always won the school races. Dan was knocked to the ground. "Gee whiz, of all people, why did I have to run into Speedy Seedy," Dan muttered under his breath, rolling his big brown eyes.

Not only was Speedy Seedy one of the track stars at Clover Line Elementary School, but his father was also the Mayor of Seedington. Years before, both his uncle and his grandfather had been mayors. The Seedy family was very rich and they were also one of the first families to live in the small town. The Seedys owned so

7

much of Seedington that it was originally named after them! Because of his family's good fortune, Jason Seedy thought he was better than everyone else.

Dan stood up quickly, brushing grass and dirt off his yellow tee shirt and brown shorts. He felt his magnifying glass in his right pocket and sighed with relief that it was not broken.

Foxy was sitting behind her lemonade stand and happened to glance at the corner just as Dan and Speedy Seedy crashed into each other. She saw Speedy Seedy's red baseball cap fly through the air, and she could see that he was very angry. Foxy and Madison rushed over to help Dan. It wasn't easy for Foxy to run in her long blue dress. She also wore a string of pearls, a wide-brimmed straw hat with a pink ribbon and bow, a bright pink feather boa, long white gloves and bright red high heels, all of which were much too big for her. Madison looked adorable in a little blue cowboy hat and a bright red bow that was tied around her collar. Madison reached the corner first and began barking at Speedy Seedy. Foxy's dress

was falling off her shoulders, showing the pale pink tee shirt that she wore under her dress. She arrived just in time to hear Speedy Seedy teasing Dan.

"You'll never beat me at the Clover County Track Meet running like that!" Speedy Seedy sneered at Dan. He picked up his red baseball cap and adjusted it over his thick eyebrows and small beady eyes. "There's no way you can win wearing those old running shoes!"

Foxy was one of the few kids who stood up to Speedy Seedy, and he did not like her for this reason. She clenched her gloved fists and replied angrily, "We'll just see about that, Jason Seedy. Just because you have the best running shoes that money can buy doesn't mean you will win the race!"

Speedy Seedy turned his head and laughed at both of them. "Both of you are jealous of me!" he said as he jabbed his finger into Dan's chest. He ran down the street, stopped, turned around, and hollered out to them: "Dan Delion, always cryin'! Dan Delion, always cryin'!" He turned the corner and was gone from sight.

9

Both Dan and Foxy were glad to see him leave. Dan didn't want to start a fight, and neither did Foxy. Even Madison seemed happy, as she quit barking as soon as he was gone from sight.

Madison trotted over to Dan and began wagging her tail. "I really want to win the Clover County Track Meet," Dan said to Foxy as he bent down to scratch Madison behind her short taffy-coloured ears.

The track meet was in less than two weeks. There were a total of five elementary schools in Seedington, and the top two runners from each grade would race against each other. That meant there would be ten students from each grade in each race. In Dan's class, Speedy Seedy placed first and Dan placed second, so they were both eligible to run in the Clover County Track Meet. Speedy Seedy earned his nickname last year when he placed first.

"You still have lots of days to practise. Don't worry, you'll win the race," Foxy said to Dan. "Just because Jason Seedy won last year doesn't mean he will win again this year. He

has been bragging to everyone in class that he's going to win the race without practising. He's also been bragging about having the best running shoes in town."

"Maybe he's right," Dan replied. "He does have the best running shoes and he is really fast. He didn't get his nickname for being a slowpoke."

"It's not fair if that bully wins. Jason is always mean to us and I wish everyone wasn't afraid of him," Foxy said. "Just because his family is rich, and his dad is the Mayor, he thinks he can do whatever he likes. Last week he was making fun of Johnny Jump-Ups and calling him names. Did you hear about that?"

"Yes, I heard about that," Dan replied. "And I don't think it's fair if he wins either."

As they walked back to Foxy's lemonade stand, Dan suddenly remembered that he had not told Foxy his big secret. "Foxy, I have a totally awesome secret to tell you," he said. "Wait until you hear what happened to me this morning!"

CHAPTER 3
COULD THIS BE TRUE?

Foxy picked up her red shoes on the way to the lemonade stand, Madison following close at her heels. "What secret? I love secrets! Tell me!" Foxy exclaimed, as she straightened out her blue-flowered dress and pulled up her long white gloves.

Once they reached the lemonade stand, Dan told Foxy his big secret. Foxy stared at him, listening to every word. She couldn't believe it!

"I think we should go to Holly's house," Foxy said, as she leaned in closer to Dan. "She just called me, so I know she's already home from the mall." Foxy quickly flipped her *Open* sign to *Closed* and slipped on a pair of running shoes that she kept under her chair. This was no time to be wearing high heels that were much too big!

They ran to Holly's house and found her sitting on the front porch with her mother, surrounded by shopping bags. Not only was Holly the tallest girl in the entire school, she was even taller than her teacher, Mr. Findlay! Sometimes she felt awkward about her height and she hunched her shoulders.

"Hello, Mrs. Hocks," Foxy and Dan chimed together. Madison ran to Holly, who was wearing a new pair of white sunglasses tucked into her hair on top of her head. She wore a blue denim jacket, a pale green tee shirt and pink shorts. Madison wagged her tail as she jumped up to lick Holly on her cheek.

"Hello Dan! Hello Foxy! Nice to see you both," Mrs. Hocks replied.

"Mrs. Hocks, may I please have a glass of milk?" Dan asked. He loved milk and he drank at least eight glasses every day.

Mrs. Hocks returned and handed Dan a tall glass of milk. "Dan, with the amount of milk that you drink, your family is going to need to buy a cow! And, Dan Delion, I can't believe how much you have grown. I swear,

every time I see you, you seem to have grown taller!"

"I know," Dan said. "Everyone's always telling me that I'm growing like a weed! Pretty soon I'll be taller than Holly!"

"You've only got a couple of inches to grow before you are taller than Holly. And that reminds me, Dan, I have some weeds to pull in the garden. Please excuse me," Mrs. Hocks said as she walked around to the backyard.

"Holly! We're so glad you are home from the mall. Wait until you hear Dan's big secret."

"What is it?" Holly asked as she arched her thin brown eyebrows.

Dan shared his secret with Holly, who stared back at him in disbelief. Her big blue eyes were opened wide. "Could this really be true," she asked herself as she twirled a lock of her long dark hair. "Dan, look, you've given me goose bumps!" Holly exclaimed as she held out her arm.

"We have to find Johnny and tell him too," Dan said. "Where should we look first?"

"Well, it is lunchtime," Holly replied.

All three looked at each other and shouted "Burger World!" at the same time. They laughed as they walked toward the popular restaurant in search of Johnny Jump-Ups.

CHAPTER 4
THREE TOMBSTONES

They spotted Johnny through the large picture window of the Burger World restaurant. He was biting into a giant hamburger. Madison waited outside while they entered the restaurant and walked over to Johnny's table.

"Hey, what's up?" Johnny asked with a huge grin, as he wiped ketchup off of his full round face with the back of his hand. Some of the ketchup fell onto his purple and yellow striped tee shirt and brown pants. "Oops!" he said, as he rubbed the stains with his napkin.

Holly looked to the left and then to the right, making sure no one was listening. "Dan has a totally awesome secret," Holly whispered.

The waitress came over and asked if anyone needed anything. Dan ordered a glass

of milk and Holly and Foxy asked for a glass of water.

"What's the big secret?" Johnny asked, raising his purple eyebrows as he took another bite of his hamburger.

The waitress plunked down their drinks. Once she left, everyone looked eagerly at Dan. He took a deep breath and began telling his secret for the third time that day.

"When I woke up this morning, I wanted to go hunting for bugs, and of course I took my magnifying glass with me. I went to that old mansion with the cemetery that's up at the top of the hill. You all know the stories about the English Ivys. It's the house they used to live in."

"Why did everyone always call the people who lived there the English Ivys?" Foxy asked.

"I know why," answered Holly. "My mom told me that their last name was Ivy and they were from England. Because they were English, everyone called them the English Ivys. She also told me that a vine called English ivy grew all over their house. Everyone thought

19

that was funny, because they had the same name as the vine!"

Johnny gasped after he swallowed a mouthful of fries. "Everyone knows that place is haunted. I hope you didn't go to the cemetery. Why would anybody want to live in a weird house like that? It's scary enough to give Virginia Creeper the creeps!"

"Everyone in my class always talks about her," Holly said. "She *is* kind of creepy, with her long black hair. She has really dark eyes, and there are always dark circles underneath them. She has bright red lips, and her ears are small and really pointed. I have never seen ears like that before. For the last two months she's been wearing black clothes every day. No one knows why. And, last week, she told our class that she saw a small ghost at the English Ivys' house."

"Virginia Creeper!" Foxy, Johnny and Dan all groaned at the same time. "Why were you talking to that gossip girl?" Johnny asked. "Geez! She pops up everywhere and she's always creeping around!"

20

"I also ran into her at the mall last week. She was with her mother, and they said hello. I was surprised that her mother had an English accent," Holly added.

"Why would Virginia Creeper go to the English Ivys' house?" Dan asked. "And we all know there is no such thing as a ghost."

"Don't be so sure," Johnny answered. "I've heard lots of haunted stuff about the English Ivys. My Dad told me that some people think that the ghost of Mrs. Ivy lives there. But I forget why."

"Yes," Foxy replied. "My mom told me that they had a little girl who died. Do you think it was her ghost that Virginia Creeper saw?"

"I guess it could be her ghost," Johnny said. "My dad told me that after the little girl died, the English Ivys were so sad that they didn't take care of their house or anything. The house has always been empty because people were afraid that it was haunted, so they didn't want to buy it. The English Ivys and their little girl were buried in their own cemetery."

"I see," Dan said. "So that's why there are

three tombstones in the front yard."

"Geez!" Johnny said. "That's scary enough for me!"

CHAPTER 5
THE MAGICAL LADYBUG

The waitress came back to their table to see if they needed anything else. Dan finished his milk and ordered another glass. Once the waitress had left, Johnny asked Holly if she thought Virginia Creeper really saw a ghost at the English Ivys' mansion.

"I don't know," Holly answered. "I only know what she told our class. She is kind of weird, but sometimes she's nice too."

"Whatever," Dan said as he interrupted Holly. "Who cares about Virginia Creeper and ghost stories? I should finish telling my secret! Anyway, I don't believe anything that Virginia Creeper says. I don't think that house is haunted. I have never seen a ghost there before."

"What happened next?" Johnny asked, anxious to hear Dan's secret.

23

"I walked by the tombstones and went around to the backyard," Dan continued as he took another gulp of milk. "I went there because I knew I would find lots of bugs. There are so many flowers and plants that grow there. That backyard is like a jungle!"

Dan looked at his friends and lowered his voice. "Anyway, I was looking for bugs, and I did find this one bug that was green with black spots on his back and . . ."

"Dan Delion!" Foxy Gloves shouted. "Forget about the green bug. Johnny is waiting to hear the really good part of your secret."

"It's okay," Johnny said with a grin. "I like hearing about bugs."

"Well, Dan's secret is, like, way better than finding green bugs," Holly replied.

"Okay," Dan said. "I stopped to rest under this really big tree. I happened to look up, and I saw something white sticking out of the top of the branches of a tall bush. I went over to see what it was, and you'll never guess in a million years what I found."

"What?" Johnny asked, as he slurped down

24

the rest of his chocolate milkshake. He moved the streak of yellow hair out of his eye with his other hand.

"I found an old greenhouse!" Dan exclaimed. "And what happened to me next was totally awesome and really scary."

They were sitting on the edge of their seats in Burger World, leaning in as close as they possibly could to hear what Dan had to say next. You would never have known that Holly and Foxy had already heard Dan's secret, as they listened carefully, gripping the table.

"This is the really good part!" Foxy cried out in excitement.

Dan's heart began thumping in his chest. "I found a shovel lying on the ground. I used it to clear away some of the bushes and weeds to get to the greenhouse. It took me about two hours to make a path. The greenhouse door was a little bit sticky, but I was finally able to pull it open."

"Then what happened?" Johnny said, chewing on his hamburger. "Did you fight off all of the ghosts with your shovel?" he joked, as

he poked a make-believe shovel around in the air.

"Whatever," Dan replied while Foxy and Holly both giggled. "I walked into the greenhouse. It was really messy. There were, like, broken flowerpots, pieces of glass, dead plants and piles of dirt all over the greenhouse floor. The glass walls were so dirty that you could not see through them, and a lot of the glass was broken. There were some benches that were broken too. Suddenly, I saw a ladybug crawling along one of the benches."

"A ladybug?" Johnny asked, creasing his purple eyebrows. "You mean a red ladybug with black spots? What's so special about a ladybug?"

"When I saw this ladybug, I was really scared. My heart was beating like crazy," Dan said, while holding his hand on his heart.

"What do you mean? Why were you scared of a ladybug?" Johnny asked. "You've never been afraid of a bug before."

Suddenly Johnny stood up from the table. He put his hand on his heart and said in a

high-pitched girl's voice, "Help me! Help me! I have just seen a scary ladybug!" Johnny slumped back down in his chair while the others laughed.

"This wasn't a normal red ladybug with black spots. Something about this ladybug was weird, but I couldn't figure out what it was. So I took my magnifying glass out of my pocket to get a closer look," Dan said, taking his magnifying glass out of his right pocket. "I let the ladybug crawl up my finger and I held it up to my face. I blew on it because I wanted to see what it would look like with its wings open. What happened next was totally scary," Dan said. "I was scared half to death."

CHAPTER 6
GLITTERING RAINBOWS

Dan leaned in close again so that no one else in the restaurant could hear him. Their heads were pressed together in the centre of the table. "The ladybug flew off my finger and left a trail of colourful sparkling glitter. It was so cool! This glitter was every colour you can think of. It looked like a rainbow! The ladybug landed in front of me. And then, all of a sudden, the ladybug got really big. It was, like, as big as my basketball!" Dan said, with his big brown eyes widening in excitement.

"C'mon. You're making this up," Johnny said, chewing on some fries. "Either that, or you're crazy."

"I am not making this up. Cross my heart! I'm not crazy, either. You can come with me to the greenhouse to see for yourself."

28

"What do you mean, I can see for myself?" Johnny asked as he raised his hands in the air. "See what? A ladybug?"

"Oh, you'll want to see this ladybug," Dan replied. "This ladybug had a small black face with two large black eyes and really long eyelashes. She had these two antennae near her eyes, a tiny little nose and very bright red lips. Her back was bright red and covered with black spots. She had six long legs. Two of her legs were at the back of her body on either side. Two were in the middle of her back, and two more were up at the front of her body. She opened her wings, and a red cape with black spots shot out of her back and flapped in the air as she flew around the greenhouse leaving the sparkly things everywhere. She zoomed around and wherever she landed, flowers and stuff magically appeared. These plants grew right in front of me! All of the broken things disappeared! It was so sweet!"

"What did you do next?" Johnny asked, not sure if he truly believed Dan's story.

"Well," Dan paused. "The ladybug started

to talk to me in a friendly voice! She knew I was scared, and she wanted me to know that everything was okay. She had a really cool voice."

"Now I know you're crazy!" Johnny said, raising his arms up in the air once again.

"I swear and cross my heart that all of this is true. She told me that her name was Lucinda the Ladybug and that she had been living in the greenhouse for a very long time. She came from London, England, and she sailed over on a cruise ship with the English Ivys. She said that the English Ivys always travelled by cruise ship because Mr. Ivy was afraid of flying. She followed them home to the mansion on Mrs. Ivy's coat. She was very happy to see that they had a greenhouse, and she said that she has lived in it ever since. The English Ivys didn't even know that she lived in their greenhouse. They never got to meet her! And, wait till you hear this! She said that she has special seeds for us to grow. I'm not sure, but I think they might be some kind of, like, magic seeds!"

"Maybe this ladybug knows if there are ghosts at the mansion!" Foxy said excitedly.

31

Suddenly someone tapped Holly on the shoulder and caught her by surprise. Holly screamed and jumped up from the table, banging into Virginia Creeper, who was standing directly behind her.

"Virginia Creeper!" Holly cried out as she stared at Virginia's dark eyes. "Why would you scare me like that?"

"I'm sorry, Holly. I only wanted to come over and say hi." As usual, Virginia was dressed in black, adding to her creepiness. "I didn't mean to scare you. What are you talking about anyway?"

Dan wanted to say *"none of your business,"* but instead he looked at Virginia's small pointy ears and said, "I was telling them about the bugs I found today." He continued to stare at her ears, thinking to himself that they were really weird.

"Well, that sounds boring to me. But, I do have some interesting news to tell you! I heard that Jason Seedy broke a track record at school yesterday. You probably already knew that, right Dan? See you at school on Monday,

Holly." Virginia turned around and suddenly vanished through the exit door.

"Sorry I screamed. I guess I was a bit creeped out after hearing about strange ladybugs and ghosts," Holly said to her friends. "I didn't think someone would tap me on the shoulder. Dan, is Virginia right about Speedy Seedy? Did he really break a record yesterday?"

"I don't know," Dan replied.

"Well, I don't always believe what Virginia says," Holly answered. "It might not be true. She gets things mixed up, so who knows what happened. She loves to gossip."

"Yes she does," Johnny piped up. "You can pass on any message by 'telephone,' 'telegram,' and 'tell a Creeper'!"

Dan almost fell out of his chair laughing. Foxy and Holly laughed so hard they had tears.

"I think Virginia is kind of icky too," Foxy added as she wiped away her tears with a gloved hand. "She's gone, so tell us the rest of your story."

"When I saw Lucinda the Ladybug fly

34

around the greenhouse with all of that glitter, well, it was the most awesome thing I have ever seen in my life! I don't know why, but I wasn't scared any more. I looked at the sparkly stuff under my magnifying glass too. Each sparkle looked like a flower, and they were all different colours. It's hard to explain. They looked the same but they were different."

"Snowflakes are like that!" Holly exclaimed as she adjusted the white sunglasses on top of her head. "If you look at them real close, you can see that each little snowflake is different."

"I never thought of that, but you're right, Holly," Dan answered. "I remember looking at snowflakes with my magnifying glass! Anyway, when I was at the greenhouse, Lucinda the Ladybug asked me to bring my best friends back this afternoon at three o'clock."

"What are we waiting for?" Foxy cried out. "Let's get going!"

CHAPTER 7
MEET LUCINDA

They left Burger World and walked toward the ivy-covered red brick mansion at the top of the hill. Madison was waiting outside the exit door and trotted happily beside Foxy. The terrier looked really cute in the little blue cowboy hat and red bow. They were anxious to get to the greenhouse and they started to run. Johnny was panting for air and had a hard time keeping up with them. They slowed down and walked instead.

"Haunted or not, I'll take my chances," Johnny said. "I won't believe any of this until I see this ladybug with my own eyes."

"It's almost two-thirty now, so let's walk faster!" Holly cried out with excitement.

"Wait a minute," Dan shouted as he held up his hand for everyone to stop. "We need to

36

keep this a secret. We can't tell anyone!" They all began to talk at the same time.

"Why don't we form a secret club?" Holly asked.

"Awesome! Oh, I know!" Dan replied excitedly. "Let's call our secret club The Greenhouse Kids. And our clubhouse can be the hidden greenhouse."

"That's sweet!" Foxy said, as Holly nodded in agreement. They locked arms and each one swore to keep Lucinda the Ladybug and the hidden greenhouse a secret.

"Let's hope that Virginia Creeper doesn't find out about this. It will be all over school and on the six o'clock news," Foxy giggled.

"No kidding," Holly laughed. "Whatever you do, don't 'tell a Creeper'!"

"C'mon," Foxy said, still giggling at Holly's joke. "I can't wait to get there!"

"Me too," Holly replied.

They arrived at the greenhouse and found that it was just as Dan had told them. The greenhouse was about twelve feet wide and twenty feet long. The metal frame was

painted white, and the roof and walls were made of shiny panes of glass. They could see large plants and brightly coloured flowers through the glass, and it looked beautiful.

"Let me go in first, and the rest of you can follow," Dan said. He peeked into the greenhouse and then slowly entered. Foxy went in next, followed by Johnny and Holly. They were quite nervous, not knowing what to expect. They stayed close to the door and to each other. Holly gasped as she walked into the greenhouse. It was even nicer than she thought it would be.

"Where is Lucinda the Ladybug?" Johnny whispered to Dan, while his small brown eyes searched the greenhouse in every direction.

"I don't see any ladybugs either," Holly quivered while she looked around nervously.

Suddenly colourful sparks appeared in the air. "There she is!" Dan said excitedly, pointing toward the end wall of the greenhouse.

Holly, Foxy, and Johnny stood frozen with their mouths gaping open in awe. Their hearts were pounding in their chests as their eyes

followed the sparkling trail. The dazzling glitter zoomed back and forth and all around them. They looked at each other in amazement, and began to shake the colourful glitter that had fallen out of their hair and clothing.

Finally, the sparkly trail stopped on a large banana plant leaf in front of them. The Greenhouse Kids were speechless as they saw Lucinda the Ladybug for the first time. And, just as Dan had told them, she suddenly began to grow to the size of a basketball!

"Hi, Lucinda!" Dan said with a big smile. The others watched with jitters, wondering what would happen next. "I would like you to meet my friends. First, I want you to meet my very best friend, Johnny Jump-Ups."

"Pleased to meet you, Johnny Jump-Ups," Lucinda the Ladybug replied in a friendly voice.

Johnny jumped back in shock. "P-p-p-pleased to m-m-m-meeet you t-t-t-too," he stammered.

Foxy and Holly were a bit frightened and they linked their arms together. "And this is

Foxy Gloves and Holly Hocks," Dan said.

"Pleased to meet you, Foxy Gloves and Holly Hocks," she said in the same soft voice. Foxy and Holly looked like they were in a daze and neither one could speak. They could only nod their heads up and down while staring wide-eyed at the ladybug in front of them.

"I must tell you a secret," Lucinda the Ladybug said. "I already knew all of your names."

"How did you know our names?" Dan asked Lucinda the Ladybug in awe.

CHAPTER 8
FLOWER POWER

Lucinda the Ladybug sat on the large banana leaf with her back legs crossed. "As soon as you were born, I knew that one day you would find me," Lucinda the Ladybug began. "All of you are extra special because you were named after a flower or plant. Now, there are many people in the world who are named after flowers and plants, but there are not very many extra special people like each one of you who have both a first and a last name that matches a flower or plant. And, most importantly, you also have things in common with the flowers or plants that you were named after. It is only the extra special people like you who are able to see me and grow my special seeds."

They all looked at Lucinda the Ladybug and were puzzled. "But how did you know

DANDELION

our names? How did you know when we were born?" Dan asked.

"On the day that you were born, your name was spelled out to me in my trail of glitter," Lucinda the Ladybug replied. "My glitter tells me whenever someone extra special is born by spelling out the name of the flower or plant that is the same as their name. That is how I knew you would find me one day."

"It's true! Look at Dan Delion," she said, as she suddenly zoomed around the greenhouse. The twinkling glitter followed her, spelling out

42

Dandelion in bright yellow glimmering letters. Everyone turned to look at Dan. Holly looked up and read Dan's name out loud, *dan-de-lion.* Suddenly they realized that he was named after the weed, dandelion.

"Hey," Dan exclaimed. "I do have things in common with a dandelion! No wonder everyone always tells me that I'm growing like a weed!"

"That's right," replied Lucinda the Ladybug. "Have you noticed that Dan also looks like a dandelion? He is tall and thin and he has a head full of spiky blonde hair that looks just like the yellow flower top of the dandelion! Have you ever picked a dandelion stem, and noticed a milky sap?"

"Yes," Dan said. "I've had that milky sap on my hands before. I remember picking dandelions with Foxy. After we picked the dandelions, we pulled off the yellow flowers. Then we linked the stems together to make her a long necklace. Do you remember, Foxy?"

"Yes, I remember!" Foxy exclaimed. "Our hands got brown spots on them from that

43

dandelion milk!"

"That is why you love milk, Dan! Just like the dandelion stem, you need milk to grow too," Lucinda explained.

"Oh!" Holly replied. "Dan also loves the colour yellow, just like a dandelion!"

HOLLYHOCKS

"Yes, Holly, you're right!" She turned to Holly and asked, "Have you ever heard of a garden flower named hollyhocks?" They all stared at Holly. "Hollyhocks are very tall pretty flowers. They stand so tall that sometimes they

droop," Lucinda the Ladybug said. "They come in many colours, and pink and crimson are popular shades."

"No wonder I love wearing pink!" Holly exclaimed, her rosy pink cheeks beaming. "And no wonder I'm so tall," she said as she threw back her hunched shoulders and tried to stand up straight. "I'll try not to let my shoulders droop."

The Greenhouse Kids looked at Holly and realized how pretty she was. They had also noticed that sometimes her shoulders did droop, just as Lucinda the Ladybug had said.

"Johnny Jump-Ups are short charming purple and yellow flowers, just like you, Johnny! They are part of the viola plant family, and they spread very easily. Your hair is so dark that it appears purple, except for that yellow streak over your ear. And your eyebrows look purple too! Johnny Jump-Ups are also known for their smiling faces. Haven't you noticed that Johnny is always smiling, and that his purple eyebrows make him look happy?"

JOHNNY JUMP-UPS

Johnny looked at all of his friends with a huge grin on his round pudgy face. "I am short, and I know that I weigh more than I should. I guess I am spreading out too, just like the flower," Johnny joked. They shared a laugh with their charming good-natured friend.

"What about me?" Foxy asked, twirling her pearl necklace between her fingers.

"You are named after an old-fashioned garden flower, foxgloves," Lucinda the Ladybug replied.

"That's funny," Foxy replied. "My real

FOXGLOVES

name is Fox, but everyone always called me Foxy. My mother said she named me Fox because of my red hair!"

"Foxgloves are creamy white and pink garden flowers that look like they have freckles across the inside of their petals. They only bloom every other year, and that is why you are so small," Lucinda the Ladybug explained. "You just don't grow as quickly as other flowers and plants do. Foxy, you are what we call a late bloomer!"

"We can see that Foxy is short and that she

47

has freckles, but why does she dress up all the time?" Holly asked.

"Many children used to play dress-up with foxgloves," Lucinda the Ladybug answered. "Children picked the flowers and placed them over their fingers to make puppets. Quite often they would dress up and put on shows with the puppets that they made. Foxgloves are old-fashioned garden flowers, and that is why she likes to dress up in old-fashioned clothes. Have you noticed that she always wears her long white gloves? You see, it only makes sense that Foxy Gloves would love to wear gloves."

Now they understood why she always wore white gloves! It was part of her name! They also understood why she liked to dress up in old clothes. They looked at the outfits that both Foxy and Madison were wearing and giggled.

"I have always loved puppets and dressing up in old clothes," Foxy admitted, using a gloved hand to wipe some red curls off of her forehead. "And, Madison likes to dress up too, don't you, girl?" Foxy said, scratching Madison

on her neck. Madison answered back with two barks and a big wet kiss on Foxy's gloved hand. The Greenhouse Kids laughed, along with Lucinda the Ladybug.

"And now, I have another surprise for all of you," Lucinda the Ladybug announced.

"I don't know if I can take any more surprises today," Johnny said, placing a hand over his heart. "I think I've had enough surprises for one day!"

"C'mon, don't be a baby," Foxy teased. She turned to Lucinda the Ladybug and smiled. "What is it?"

Suddenly, Lucinda the Ladybug whirled around the greenhouse, her red cape flapping in the air. The greenhouse was magically filled with flowerpots, bags of soil, garden tools, watering cans, aprons, garden clogs and garden gloves.

"Wow, I have never seen anything like that before," Holly said in awe. The others stood frozen in place, and could only nod their heads up and down.

"As I explained earlier, only the extra

special people like you, who are fully named after flowers or plants, are able to see me and grow my special seeds," Lucinda the Ladybug told them. "Please put on your aprons, clogs and garden gloves."

"Oh, I get it!" exclaimed Holly. "Your special seeds are the second part of the surprise! Now that you have given us these aprons and things, we are going to get some special seeds to grow. Is that right?" Holly asked, her big blue eyes shining with excitement.

CHAPTER 9
LUCINDA'S SEEDS

They could not believe what had happened to them! And now there would be special seeds to grow! Lucinda the Ladybug did not tell them all of her secrets, though. She was going to give each one of them a special seed that would benefit them personally, or help with a problem that they had at home or school. She already knew what they would ask for, but she did not share this with them. She wanted each one of them to tell her what they wanted to grow, and why.

"Dan," Lucinda the Ladybug said. "Tell me something. If you could grow anything that would help you at home or school, what would it be? Or, perhaps you have a problem that you need help with?"

"That's easy!" Dan replied at once. "I need

51

something that could make me run faster. And it has to grow quick, because I have the Clover County Track Meet in less than two weeks. I really want to beat this boy in my class, Jason Seedy! He runs so fast that his nickname is Speedy Seedy."

"Tell me more about the track meet and this boy named Speedy Seedy," Lucinda the Ladybug said to Dan, even though she already knew everything there was to know about Jason Seedy.

Dan told her that they already had a race at school, and that Speedy Seedy had placed first and he had placed second. He explained that they would both race at the Clover County Track Meet along with the two best runners from each school in Seedington. Since there were four other elementary schools, there would be ten students from each grade in each race.

"Speedy Seedy is also the school bully and he likes to pick on us. He's very mean," Foxy added. "Dan forgot to tell you that."

"I see," said Lucinda the Ladybug, raising

52

one of her long front legs to scratch her head. She began tapping her mouth with the other front leg as she thought quietly for a moment.

"I think Dan would have won last year, but he caught a bad cold," Johnny piped up. "He was sick for a week and almost missed the race."

"Whatever. Forget about last year," Dan replied. He looked at Lucinda the Ladybug and asked, "Do you have any special seeds that would help me win the race?"

Lucinda the Ladybug continued to tap her long leg against her mouth while thinking. "I think I have just the seeds for you, Dan."

"Oh, what are they?" he asked excitedly, imagining magical powers that would make his legs run faster.

"I am going to give you carrot seeds. Yes, I am sure you should grow carrots," she replied.

"Carrots?" Dan asked, with a puzzled look on his face. "How are they going to help me run faster?"

"Carrots are full of vitamins and they are one of the best vegetables that you can eat,"

Lucinda the Ladybug answered. "They also contain carbohydrates to give you extra energy. Luckily, I planted carrots earlier, and you can begin eating my special carrots right away. Here are some you can munch on now. We will plant some carrot seeds later, and you will have many more for future races too."

She scooped a few super-sized carrots from the lower shelf of the greenhouse bench and handed them to Dan. "Look how big these carrots are!" he exclaimed. "I have never seen carrots like this! These carrots are almost the same size as my baseball bat. Awesome! Thanks, Lucinda!" Dan said, while biting into one of the carrots. He couldn't wait to start eating them every day!

"Gee," Johnny said. "I'm hungry too. Can I have one of those carrots to eat?"

"Of course you can have one. Carrots are good for everyone," she said, handing each one of them a huge carrot. A packet of carrot seeds suddenly floated in the air and she tossed them to Dan. She also gave him a few more carrots that he could take home. She reminded

him that there were plenty more, if he happened to run out.

"There is one thing you must remember, Dan," warned Lucinda the Ladybug. "You can't only eat the carrots and expect to win the race. You must work hard and practise running every day. And you have to believe in yourself too!"

Dan knew how lucky he was to have these magical carrots! "Lucinda, I promise! And thanks again!"

"You are very welcome," she replied.

Foxy was putting on the red apron and blue clogs that had magically appeared in front of her. "I know what I want to grow!" she exclaimed to Lucinda the Ladybug. "I have a lemonade stand at my house. If I could grow my own lemons, I could make more money because I could sell the lemons too. And I wouldn't have to buy the lemons at the store to make my lemonade."

"What are you planning on doing with the extra money that you will receive?" Lucinda the Ladybug asked.

"I am going to save half of the money to buy Christmas presents. I am going to spend the other half on some stuff I saw at the mall."

"It's very nice of you to save half of the money for Christmas gifts, Foxy," Lucinda the Ladybug said.

Suddenly a packet of lemon tree seeds sliced through the air and landed in Foxy's apron pocket.

"These are very special lemon tree seeds," she explained to Foxy. "The seeds will grow very quickly, so you will not have to wait long before you have delicious, ripe lemons."

Foxy thanked Lucinda the Ladybug, as she began to dream about all of the lemonade she would be selling over the summer. She also thought about all the things she would be able to buy at the mall!

"Could I please grow huge giant sunflowers that are even taller than I am?" Holly wanted to know. "My mother always had a garden in our backyard, and she used to grow them. I always liked to stand beside them because they were taller than I was!"

"Why, of course you may," Lucinda the Ladybug said. "Check your pocket."

"Are you sure you don't want to grow cotton?" joked Johnny. "That way you could make all of your clothes instead of buying them at the mall!"

"Whatever," Holly said as she giggled along with the others. She reached into her apron pocket and was stunned to find a packet of giant sunflower seeds. "Thanks, Lucinda. I can't wait to grow these!"

Johnny was smiling. He knew in an instant what he wanted to grow. "I have always wanted to grow my own pumpkins for Halloween. That would be so cool! I could make jack-o'-lanterns for everyone. And my mom could make me pumpkin pies! I love Halloween!"

"As you wish," Lucinda the Ladybug replied, as a packet of pumpkin seeds suddenly floated back and forth, in mid-air, right in front of Johnny's face.

"Wow! Thanks, Lucinda," Johnny exclaimed as he reached up and plucked the seed packet from thin air.

CHAPTER 10
PROMISES

They gathered around Lucinda the Ladybug, chattering excitedly about growing their seeds. "There is something else that you need to know," Lucinda the Ladybug told them. They looked up at her, anxious to hear what she had to say. "I will teach you how to grow your seeds, but you must take care of them yourselves every day. All plants and flowers must be watered and cared for, or they will die."

"Gee, I can't let my magical carrots die," Dan said. "Don't worry. We promise that we will take care of our plants every day. We will need your help, because we don't know what to do."

"I'll be happy to help you," she replied.

They stood in a circle with their arms

linked together. Lucinda the Ladybug flew around The Greenhouse Kids. They were in awe as they watched her circling above them. They looked up and saw their names in brilliant letters! *Dandelion* glistened in bright yellow, *Hollyhocks* sparkled in pink and crimson, *Foxgloves* glowed in pale pink and *Johnny Jump-Ups* twinkled in purple and bright yellow!

"I feel like I'm standing in the middle of a rainbow!" Holly said in disbelief.

They promised that they would take care of their plants. Dan spoke for all of them. "We, The Greenhouse Kids, promise that we will take care of our plants every day."

"We promise!" the others added.

"That's great," Lucinda the Ladybug said as she sat down on a nearby rose petal. "Planting seeds is easy and it is fun too. We'll have to wait until tomorrow. It's time for your supper and you need to go home. We can meet here after breakfast tomorrow."

"Yes, I do have to go home for supper," Foxy replied.

"I'm starving," Johnny said, patting his stomach.

"Thanks, Lucinda, and we'll see you tomorrow," Dan said.

"Yes, Lucinda, thank you," Foxy added.

Holly and Johnny also thanked her. The Greenhouse Kids were very excited as they walked out of the greenhouse toward the cemetery.

"Look at all the dark clouds in the sky!" Foxy exclaimed. "It was so sunny a few hours ago. Now, it's kind of dark out. They don't have any street lights up here either."

They walked toward the road. The pine trees whistled in the wind, making eerie sounds. The ivy vines on the old mansion waved in the breeze, giving the house a very spooky appearance.

"It's a bit darker, but it's no big deal," Dan replied. "The house doesn't scare me and it's only the wind making those sounds that we hear. Johnny, you should have seen how scared you were!" he said as he suddenly fell to the ground laughing, his carrots scattered around him.

"Well, it's not every day that I meet a giant talking ladybug!" Johnny replied.

"That's true," Holly said. She knew that Johnny did not want to tell them that he was scared.

"I was afraid myself," Foxy piped up. "I would like to get away from these tombstones! This place gives me the creeps. *And* it looks like it's going to rain!"

Suddenly a bolt of lightning cracked through the gloomy sky, startling them. Dan picked himself up off the ground and gathered his carrots. "Let's get going! Let's make sure that no one follows us too."

"Especially Virginia Creeper," Holly said. "And you know how she pops up everywhere. We need to be really careful."

"Let's make sure we keep our eyes open on the way home," Johnny said as they all began to look around. "Luckily, we've got Madison with us!"

They thought that nobody saw them, but they were wrong. Had they looked up at the mansion's second-storey window with the

broken shutter, they would have seen a shadow hiding behind the white curtains.

CHAPTER 11
THE SECRET TUNNEL

They made it to the bottom of the hill without seeing anyone. "Well, here's my street," Foxy said as giant raindrops began to fall.

"Wait," Holly said. "We might be able to find out more about the English Ivys by going to the library. It's open until eight o'clock tonight. I can ask my parents if they know anything too."

"Yes, we could ask the librarian, Miss Mercer, to help us. She's really cool. Maybe we could find something out on the Internet!" Dan exclaimed. "Let's meet there after supper."

"I think we should look up our names on the Internet too. It would be fun to see what the flowers and plants that we're named after look like!" Holly said with excitement in her voice. "We all know what a dandelion

63

looks like, but I am not sure about the rest of us! And, we won't need to bother Miss Mercer. We can search the Internet for our own names!"

"I can't wait!" Foxy said as she waved goodbye. "Let's go before we get soaked!"

"See ya," the others replied as they waved goodbye and ran home in the rain.

After supper, Holly ran next door to Dan's house. The rain had stopped and they walked to the library, jumping over every puddle that crossed their path. When they arrived, Foxy and Johnny were already huddled around a computer with Miss Mercer, telling her that they were working on a secret project and that they wanted to find out everything they could about the English Ivys.

"Don't worry. I can keep a secret, and I would love to help you out," Miss Mercer said as she winked and adjusted her dark-rimmed glasses. "Does anyone know the name of the English Ivys' daughter, or when she died?" Miss Mercer asked.

"Yes," Holly replied, as she pulled a piece of paper out of her pocket to read her notes.

"My mom told me that her name was Marigold. She said that she died about twenty years ago when she was eight years old. My mom also said that a lot of people think that Mr. and Mrs. Ivy died of a broken heart about ten years later."

"Okay," Miss Mercer said. "Let's work with these dates on our Internet search. Why don't we begin by looking through the obituaries."

"Obituaries?" Foxy asked. "What's that?"

"It's a notice that is listed in the newspaper when someone dies," Miss Mercer answered. "The newspaper notice usually gives their birth date and some other personal information. Holly and Dan can search for Marigold. Johnny, you can look for Mrs. Ivy. And Foxy, you can search for Mr. Ivy."

Miss Mercer wished them luck and returned to her desk, her long blonde ponytail swinging back and forth. "Thanks, Miss Mercer!" Dan exclaimed. "Okay, let's start looking for stuff!"

Their keyboards started clacking as they began typing. Suddenly Dan shouted out with

excitement that he found something about Marigold. He began reading it to the others from his computer screen. *"Marigold Sarah Ivy, 8 years old, of London, England, now residing in Seedington, Ontario, passed away after a brief illness on Saturday, October 24, 1988. Beloved daughter of Evert and Ginger Ivy. Dearly missed by many relatives. A private graveside service has been held for the family."*

"Who are the relatives?" Foxy said. "Do you think they lived here in Seedington? Or do you think they lived in England? Maybe they live here right now!"

"My parents didn't tell me that the English Ivys had relatives. Mr. and Mrs. Ivy must have been the only ones there," Holly said. "And it didn't tell us the day that she was born. But we could figure it out. If she was eight years old when she died in 1988, then she must have been born in 1980."

"Good thinking, Holly," said Dan. "Who wants to go to the cemetery tonight and take a look around? We can write down the dates on the tombstones. Like Miss Mercer said, the

66

dates will make it easier for us to search on the Internet."

"It's okay with me," Holly answered. "Johnny and Foxy, can you go?"

"Yes," Foxy replied. "I wish Madison was coming with me. But I don't like to bring her out after supper."

Johnny finally agreed after Dan and Holly talked him into it.

"Before we leave, I want to look up "hollyhocks" to see what they look like," Holly said.

"Yes, we forgot to look up our names!" Foxy replied. "You go first, Holly."

She typed "hollyhocks" in the search bar and hit enter. "Here's a picture! Look! It says they are over six feet tall! I guess I've got a few more inches to grow! They are pink and crimson just like the sparkling letters that spelled my name in the greenhouse!"

Next, Holly typed in a search for johnny jump-ups. "Hey, Johnny, this is funny! You do look like these purple and yellow flowers!"

"Cool," Johnny replied, pleased to see his name on the computer screen.

67

"And here are the foxgloves!" Holly exclaimed. "Look! It shows a picture of kids playing with the flowers, making puppets on their fingers. And now I can see how the freckles across your nose look like the freckles on the inside of the flower!"

"That is awesome, that we all have names that are on the Internet!" Foxy said.

"Okay, let's go!" said Dan. "And remember, let's make sure no one is following us, especially Virginia Creeper! We don't have Madison with us!"

They waved goodbye to Miss Mercer and walked out of the library toward the hill. "Shouldn't we bring a flashlight, or something?" Johnny asked. "We're near Foxy's house. Foxy, do you know if you have a flashlight?"

"Sure. I know my dad has one that he keeps in the garage. I'll be back in a flash!" Foxy hollered out as she ran home. Everyone giggled at Foxy's joke.

A few minutes later, Foxy joined them with the flashlight and they began walking up

68

the hill. The further they went, the scarier it got. The gloomy skies had made the night darker than usual. The tree frogs were making loud trilling sounds, and they were surrounded by a patch of dead tree branches that looked like bony arms reaching out to snatch them. No one wanted to say that they were afraid, as they neared the top of the hill.

"We're almost there!" Dan called out. "I can see the tombstones from here!"

They walked across the front yard, arriving at the three tombstones. "Quick, where is that flashlight, Foxy?" Dan asked. "Shine it over here so we can see what it says."

"Here is Mrs. Ivy's tombstone," Foxy shouted. *"In loving memory of Ginger Isabel Ivy. July 18th, 1935 – August 6th, 1998. Loving wife of Evert Samuel Ivy. May she rest in peace beside her daughter, Marigold Sarah Ivy."*

"Shine the light over here," Johnny said. *"In loving memory of Evert Samuel Ivy. May 12, 1932 – December 11, 1998. Loving husband of Ginger Isabel Ivy. Rest in peace.* This tombstone in the middle must belong to Marigold.

Let's see what it says!" Johnny read Marigold's tombstone to them: *"Marigold Sarah Ivy. April 14, 1980 – October 24, 1988. Our Precious Little Angel, Love Forever."*

"It's so sad that she was only eight years old," Holly sighed.

"Yes it is," Foxy agreed.

"I'll write down these dates," Holly said as she took a pen and paper out of her pocket. "Look at the house!" she exclaimed. "It looks weird with those vines hanging everywhere. And, the house is so dark without any lights!"

70

The red brick mansion looked ghostly as the ivy created strange shadows and rustling sounds. The windows had shutters that were closed up, except for one on the second floor that began banging in the wind.

"What's that noise?" Johnny said in a frightened voice as he straightened his back.

"Don't worry, it's just one of the boards up there," Dan answered as he pointed to the window on the second storey. "It must be broken."

Suddenly, a door slammed! They all screamed at the same time.

"Look over there! That was the door on that old shed," Holly said, while pointing toward a shed that was mostly hidden by large bushes and pine trees.

"Funny, I've never noticed that shed before," Dan said. "Let's go look at it."

"Do we have to?" Johnny asked, his voice slightly quivering.

"Don't be a baby," Dan teased.

They walked to the shed slowly, while looking all around them. After peeking in the

71

door, Dan wanted to explore it further. As soon as they entered the dark shed, Johnny tripped and tumbled over. He reached out to break his fall, and grabbed Foxy and Holly by the legs. They both screamed at the same time, not sure what had wrapped around their legs in the dark.

"Shhhhhhh, it's just me," Johnny whispered. "I tripped over something and fell, but I'm okay."

"Foxy, can I have the flashlight?" Dan asked in a low voice. "I want to see what he tripped over. Look!" Dan said, as he scuffed his foot over a spot in the floor. "There's a trap door with a metal ring. Johnny, you must have got your foot caught in the metal ring."

"Should we try to open it?" Holly asked.

"I'll open it," Dan offered. The trap door opened easily and he shone the flashlight down into the darkness. "Look! There is a ladder and it leads down into a tunnel. The tunnel goes toward the house! I'm going down the ladder. Who is coming with me?"

"I didn't even want to come into the shed,

and now you want me to go down a dark tunnel!" Johnny said in a shaky voice. "If the rest of you are going, I am too. There is no way I am going to stay here by myself!"

Curiosity got the better of them. Dan decided to go first, followed by Holly, then Foxy. Johnny was the last one down the ladder. He was frightened and he stayed close to Foxy.

Dan shone the flashlight around the tunnel while they slowly inched their way toward the house. It was so quiet that you could have heard a pin drop. Dan shone the flashlight straight ahead. "Look!" he exclaimed. "There is a green door and it looks like it goes into the house!"

CHAPTER 12
SOMEBODY IS IN THE HOUSE

They looked at each other, trying to decide who should open the green wooden door. It looked very old and the paint was peeling off of it. "I think we should go back now," Johnny said. "This is getting way too scary."

"Stand back," Dan ordered. "I'll open it." His heart was racing, but he didn't want them to know that he was afraid too. The doorknob rattled loudly as he tried to open the door by jiggling the knob.

"The door is stuck!" Dan shouted out. "Let me try again." Dan pushed against the door with his shoulder and the door moved. "It opened a bit!" he said, as he felt around the doorframe. "I think if we all push against the door together, it will open."

"Maybe we should go home now," Foxy

said in a scared voice. "I'm not sure I want to go in there!"

"Good idea," Johnny agreed. "Who wants to go home now?"

"Don't you want to find out if this door goes into the house?" Dan asked.

"Well, why don't you go, Dan, and let us know what you find," Johnny answered, only half joking.

"C'mon," Dan said. "Let's try to push the door open. It will be fun to see what's in the house!"

They pushed on the door as hard as they could. Suddenly, the door opened. The Greenhouse Kids spilled into the house and landed on the floor, their arms and legs tangled together!

"Wow!" Holly said, as she picked herself up off the floor. "Who would have thought this house had a secret tunnel."

There were a few steps to climb, leading to an open doorway that brought them into the kitchen. "Look at this place!" Foxy exclaimed, as Dan shone the flashlight around the room.

"Everything in here is really old. This stuff must have belonged to the English Ivys."

They began to walk around the kitchen, the floorboards creaking underneath them. Some light filtered in through the cracks in the shutters, allowing them to see once they got used to the dim light. There was a living room in the house and a winding wood staircase that led to the second floor. Old flowered wallpaper was hanging off of the walls in the dining room and cobwebs hung from the old chandelier. Everything in the house was coated with a thick layer of dust and the place was covered in cobwebs. Dirty white sheets were draped over all of the furniture. The front door had a wide piece of wood nailed across it.

Dan was making his way toward the living room while the others began looking in the kitchen. Suddenly, they heard a loud crashing noise! It sounded like it was coming from upstairs! They all screamed out in fright, and their hearts pounded loudly in their chests.

"Let's get out of here!" Johnny said, and this time no one argued with him.

They ran out of the kitchen, back down the steps and into the tunnel, panicking and banging into each other. They finally made it to the ladder. Taking turns, they quickly climbed up the ladder into the shed. They looked at each other, wondering what they should do next.

"I'll go outside and take a look around. I'll be back in a minute. If I'm gone any longer than that, come and look for me!" Dan whispered, not knowing if someone was close enough to hear them.

"Oh, Dan, I don't know what we should do. What if someone is out there?" Holly whispered back.

"Well, we can't stay in this shed," Dan replied. "Maybe someone else was in the house. Maybe they're coming down the tunnel! Open the door a crack so that you can peek out and watch me."

Dan poked his head out, didn't see anything, and carefully made his way toward the tombstones. He turned to look at the dark mansion and did not see anything out of the

ordinary. Everything looked fine.

He waved toward the shed for the others to follow him. Holly, Foxy and Johnny bolted out of the shed. All four sprinted through the cemetery, and they did not stop running until they reached the road. Finally, Johnny dropped to the ground panting for air.

They sat at the edge of the road, catching their breath. They could see the house in the distance. "Look!" Foxy cried out as she pointed toward the house. They looked at the house and sucked in their breath. A flickering light was coming from a window on the second floor! It was the window with the broken shutter. Somebody else *must* have been in the house with them!

"Somebody else is in there! Let's get out of here!" Foxy said as she stood up. "I'm really scared!" They turned around and ran as fast as they could down the hill, their hearts beating wildly. Johnny was lagging behind, but he wasn't complaining.

They reached Foxy's lemonade stand safely. They couldn't wait to talk to Lucinda the

Ladybug about going into the house. Maybe she could tell them who else was in there!

"Let's meet here at the lemonade stand tomorrow after breakfast," Dan suggested.

"Good idea," Holly replied. "How about ten o'clock?"

"That sounds good," Foxy added. "I'll see you here in the morning. I can't wait!"

They said goodbye to each other and went home before it was totally dark.

Dan went to sleep early, anxious for the next day to arrive. He was up at the crack of dawn for breakfast, enjoying a carrot muffin with a glass of milk. After playing video games, Dan dressed in a pair of jeans and a bright yellow tee shirt. He ran next door to get Holly. She was waiting on the front porch, wearing a pretty pink shirt, jeans, and pink ballerina flats. Her white sunglasses were tucked into her hair on top of her head.

"Hi. I am so excited today! Remember, we have to make sure that no one is following us!" Holly reminded him as they walked to Foxy's lemonade stand. "I hope we can find out if

someone else was in the house!"

"Yes," he replied. "Maybe Lucinda the Ladybug will be able to tell us something."

Foxy, Madison, and Johnny were waiting for them. Foxy was holding her wide-brimmed straw hat and Johnny was wearing a purple and green striped shirt that hung out over his jeans.

"We thought you'd never get here!" Foxy said excitedly. "C'mon, I can't wait to get there! I have butterflies in my stomach, I am so nervous," she added as she put on her hat and twirled her pearl necklace.

"Me too," Johnny replied. "I'm really glad that Madison is with us!"

"Remember, we need to be careful. We don't want anyone to see us," Dan reminded them as they headed toward the hill. "Especially since somebody else was in the house!"

No one answered, but they were all thinking the exact same thing as they raced to their hidden greenhouse. Who could it be?

CHAPTER 13
WHISTLES AND WARNINGS

As they walked toward the mansion, Holly stopped mid-way up the hill and said, "Wait! Maybe one of us should go up ahead and make sure that no one else is around."

They all looked at Dan. "Okay, I'll go. I'll whistle three times when it's safe for you to come up."

"We'll hide behind these bushes until we hear you whistle," Foxy said as she pulled up her long white gloves and wrapped her pink boa tighter around her bright purple dress. She picked up Madison, straightened her little cowboy hat, and held her in her arms. "Be careful, Dan."

"I'll be okay, and hopefully I'll see you in a few minutes," Dan replied as he nervously walked up the hill.

Foxy held Madison tight. They crouched as low to the ground as they could, so that they were out of sight from the road.

Dan reached the top of the hill. Suddenly Virginia Creeper popped out from behind a huge maple tree directly in front of him. "Whoa!" Dan called out in surprise. He wasn't expecting to see Virginia, and she frightened him. "Virginia, what are you doing here? You scared the wits out of me!"

"Well, what are you doing here?" Virginia asked as she pushed her long wavy black hair behind her small pointed ears.

Dan rolled his big brown eyes. "Not much," he replied. He took his magnifying glass out of his pocket and said, "I'm, like, hunting for bugs. Is that a crime? So, what are you doing here?"

"Sometimes I come up here for a walk," Virginia said as she looked away. She jammed her fists into the front pockets of her black pants and walked down the hill toward Foxy, Johnny and Holly. Dan was thinking fast. How could he warn his friends that Virginia

Creeper was about to cross paths with them? Sadly, there was little he could do without Virginia becoming suspicious.

As she walked down the hill, Dan called out in a very loud voice, "See you later, Virginia Creeper." He crossed his fingers and hoped they heard his warning.

"Shhhhhh," Johnny said, holding his finger up to his mouth. "I think I heard Dan shout something. I think I hear someone coming! Foxy, I hope Madison doesn't bark!"

Foxy scratched Madison behind her ears and held her tighter. They crouched down lower, barely breathing. Their mouths gaped open in surprise as they watched Virginia Creeper walk by through an opening in the bushes. Luckily, Madison did not bark, and Virginia did not see them as she went down the gravel road.

"What was she doing up here?" Foxy asked.

"Who knows," Holly replied. "I see she was wearing black again."

"She must have seen Dan," Johnny said.

"We'll have to stay here and wait for him to whistle."

Five minutes passed, but it seemed like five days. Finally, they heard three short whistles come from the top of the hill. Carefully they came out of their hiding spot, looked back and forth on the road, and scrambled up toward Dan.

"Did you see Virginia Creeper?" Johnny asked.

"Yes, she crept up on me as usual and scared the wits out of me. She popped out from behind this big tree!" Dan replied.

"What did she say to you?" Holly asked.

"She asked me what I was doing here. I told her I was hunting for bugs. Luckily I had my magnifying glass with me, so I think she believed me," Dan said.

"That was a smart thing to say. I wonder what she was doing here," Foxy said.

"She said she was going for a walk."

"I don't believe her," Holly said. "Do you think she knows about Lucinda the Ladybug or the hidden greenhouse?"

"No, I don't think she does," Dan replied. "She would never be able to keep a secret that big!"

As they turned to walk toward the green-house, Holly exclaimed, "I hope you're right!"

CHAPTER 14
READY TO GROW

They burst through the greenhouse door, searching for Lucinda the Ladybug. Suddenly she appeared, flying around the greenhouse. She landed on a large plant leaf, grew to the size of a basketball, and asked them if they were ready to plant their seeds.

They all began talking excitedly at the same time. "My goodness!" Lucinda the Ladybug exclaimed. "Please, one at a time! What is it that has you so excited?"

"We have to talk to you about last night," Dan said. He told her everything that had happened to them and asked her what she thought.

Before she could answer, Johnny asked, "Do you think there are any ghosts up here?"

"I've never seen a ghost here. But I will

certainly keep my eyes open and let you know if I see any. Old houses have a habit of making odd noises. Quite often they creak and moan."

"What about the light in the window?" Foxy asked.

"Are you sure you saw a light? After all, you were very scared and your imaginations may have been running wild."

"Well, I was pretty sure," Foxy answered. She bent down to fix Madison's cowboy hat. "But we were really scared too."

"Do you know a girl in Holly's class named Virginia Creeper? She has long wavy black hair, bright red lips and small pointy ears. Lately, she has been wearing black clothes all the time. Have you ever seen her up here?" Johnny asked.

"Yes," Lucinda the Ladybug replied. "I know who she is, and I have seen her up here before. She doesn't know who I am though. She hasn't found this greenhouse."

"That's a relief! We think she's up to something," Holly said. "Lucinda, can you please let us know if you see her up here."

Lucinda the Ladybug agreed to let them know if she saw Virginia Creeper. "Now, how about planting those seeds?" she asked. "Dan, have you had any of your carrots yet?"

"Oh yes! I had some with my supper last night. My mother made me carrot muffins and I had one for breakfast."

"Excellent!" she replied. "Let's start planting our seeds."

"We will need help because we don't know what to do," Foxy said.

"I will gladly help you," Lucinda the Ladybug answered. "First, let's put on our aprons, clogs and garden gloves. I wouldn't want you to get your clothes dirty."

While they were putting on their aprons, she explained that all seeds are different and that it is important to read the instructions on the seed packet. "Some seeds like lots of water and some only a little bit. Most seeds like lots of sunlight, but some like to be kept in the dark. After the seeds have sprouted, the seedlings can be moved into larger flowerpots, or even planted outside in a garden, if it

is warm enough."

"How do you know which plants like to grow in the sunlight and which ones like to be kept in the dark?" Foxy asked.

"You need to look at the picture of the sun on your seed packet. The picture of the sun is like a secret code. It tells you where to plant the seeds. For example, a sun that is coloured all white or all yellow means that the seeds need to be planted where they will have the sun shining on them all day. A sun that is coloured half black means that the seeds should be planted where they will get both sunlight and shade. A sun that is coloured all black means that the seeds need to be planted in the shade only, without any sun."

"Cool," Dan replied, as the others nodded their heads in agreement.

Lucinda the Ladybug gave them each a bag of soil and small clay flowerpots. "Fill your pots almost up to the top with soil. Now, take your watering can and water the soil so that the water runs out of the holes that are underneath the flowerpot."

The Greenhouse Kids read the instructions on their seed packets to see if the seeds needed to be sprinkled on top of the soil, or buried under the soil, as Lucinda the Ladybug taught them.

"This is pretty easy," Johnny said.

"Yes, it is," Holly agreed.

Lucinda the Ladybug had already cleared one of the benches so that their seeds could sprout in the warm greenhouse. She also told them that ladybugs were a gardener's best friend because they liked to eat other bugs that could be harmful to plants. "And of course I'll be happy to eat any pests who show up to snack on your plants," she said, licking her bright red lips.

They stared at the flowerpots, feeling really good about their work. Suddenly, the seeds started to sprout! "Wow!" Dan said. "Look how fast they're growing!" They had to remind themselves that these were special seeds. They knew that real seeds must take much longer to sprout.

"I'll watch for any harmful pests while

you're in school," Lucinda the Ladybug said. "But remember, you must take good care of your plants or else they will die."

"Yes, we promised that we would," Holly replied. "Dan has to practise running after school, and as soon as he is finished, we'll come to take care of our plants."

"See you tomorrow, Lucinda," Foxy said as they went out the door and began to walk home.

They had just left the greenhouse when Johnny piped up, "What time is it anyway? I am absolutely starving!"

"You missed your lunch today!" Dan replied. "It's already five o'clock! We were so busy planting seeds that we forgot to have lunch."

"What's everyone doing later?" Johnny asked. "There's nothing on TV except for stinky reruns. Whenever I'm watching a stinky TV show, I call it smellevision!"

"Smellevision!" Holly cried out. "That's really funny!" she said as everyone laughed.

"I've got to get my homework done," Foxy said. She giggled and scooped Madison into

91

her arms. "And Madison is hungry too!"

"It won't take you long to get your home-work done, Foxy! We all know what a great memory you have," Holly replied. "I have some math homework, and I bet it'll take me a lot longer than you."

"Foxy, you always remember everything, almost word for word. I don't know how you do it. Anyway, my grandparents are coming over for supper tonight, so I'll be at home," Dan told them. "I guess I'll be watching smellevision too!" They talked about last night's events as they walked home.

"See you at school tomorrow," Foxy said as she waved goodbye.

When Dan got home he went straight to the kitchen for another carrot muffin. "Mmmmm, these are really good," he said to himself.

Chapter 15
Another Ghost

The last days of school flew by. They were so busy finishing the school year, taking care of their plants, and helping Dan to practise running that they didn't have time to get back to the library to look up the tombstone dates of the English Ivys.

Lucinda the Ladybug greeted them daily and she was very happy with the good work they were doing. They went to the greenhouse either after school or after supper every day. All of their plants were healthy and growing very well.

One evening the Greenhouse Kids were at the greenhouse, watering their plants. "I can't believe that tomorrow is my big race," Dan said nervously. "I've just had my magical carrots with my supper. I've been eating them and practising every day."

"Yes, the race is finally here, and we only have two more days of school! I can't wait to start our summer holidays. Dan, don't worry about the race. We know you're going to beat Jason," Holly said.

"Yeah, he better watch out!" Johnny chimed in. "You could beat him blindfolded!"

"Yes, you can, Dan," Foxy replied. "I don't know anyone who wants him to win."

"Wish me luck, Lucinda. We will come to the greenhouse tomorrow right after the race," Dan said.

"Goodbye and good luck," she replied. "I'll see you all tomorrow."

They left the greenhouse and cut through the cemetery. "Look! What's over there in those bushes?" Johnny said as he pointed toward a large bush.

Dan shaded his eyes with his hand and looked toward the overgrown bushes. "Johnny, I don't know what that is." Dan made his way toward the bushes and held up a white sheet. It had a piece of string wrapped around its neck, creating a head. "Somebody made this

94

ghost, and they wanted it to look like a kid!" he exclaimed. "Who would do this?"

"Do you think that this is the ghost that Virginia Creeper saw?" Holly asked. "Remember I told you that she said she saw a small ghost up here? Do you think that she thought this was the ghost of Marigold Ivy?"

"I think someone is trying to scare us," Johnny gasped. "But why would somebody want to scare us?"

"Let's leave the ghost here, so they won't know that we found it," Dan answered. "Let's get back to the library. You never know what we'll find when we search the tombstone dates!"

They walked down the hill without seeing anyone. At least, that's what they thought. But this time it was Virginia Creeper who was crouched behind the bushes, watching them go by. She crept down the hill to spy on them further, but when she reached the bottom, she wasn't sure where they had gone.

They entered the library at seven o'clock and dashed over to the computers. Miss Mercer greeted them and asked if they needed any

help. She also reminded them that the library closed in an hour. They told her the dates that they found on the tombstones. "Let's try a search on Evert and Ginger Ivy in London, England, and see what we find," Miss Mercer suggested.

"Look, here's a story about them!" Holly blurted out excitedly. "Thanks for your help, Miss Mercer; I think we are okay now."

"Glad to help you out," Miss Mercer replied as she slid her dark-rimmed glasses onto her small nose and walked to her desk.

Holly began telling them about the story she had found. "It's some kind of a newspaper story. It's dated July 5th, 1982, and it says it's about families who are moving to Canada from London, England, on a cruise ship. The story talks about the English Ivys. But look! It doesn't say anything about Marigold. That's weird, because in 1982 Marigold would have been, like, two years old! Her tombstone said she was born April 14, 1980!"

"That is weird," Foxy agreed. "Maybe the newspaper made a mistake."

"Or, maybe the English Ivys were hiding something," Dan said. "I will have to find out more about this tomorrow. I've got to get home and go to sleep. I don't want to wake up tired for the race."

Everyone wished Dan good luck as they walked home, talking excitedly about the mysterious newspaper story they had read about the English Ivys. Tomorrow was the day of the race, and the following day school was out for the summer!

Dan went to bed that night but he was so nervous that he could not fall asleep right away. Soon, though, he drifted off into a sound sleep.

CHAPTER 16
THE RACE

The following morning, Dan sprang out of bed. It was hard for him to believe that the track meet was finally here! He dressed quickly in his school uniform of royal blue shorts and a yellow jersey. He felt lucky wearing the bright yellow shirt. He hurried down to the kitchen for breakfast. His mom was making him some fresh carrot juice, and he was secretly hoping that the magical carrots would make him win the race.

Dan ran next door and he and Holly walked to school together. "Are you nervous?" Holly asked.

"A little bit," Dan replied. He was chewing his lip. "I've practised every day and I think I have a good chance of winning that race. And I have been eating those magical carrots

like crazy!"

"Dan Delion!" Holly exclaimed. "I've never heard you say that you thought you might win!"

"I've never eaten magical carrots before either." Dan replied, just as the school bell rang.

"See you at the track, and good luck!" Holly said as she waved goodbye and went to her class.

"Thanks," Dan said, and turned down a separate hallway. Suddenly Speedy Seedy appeared and shoved Dan.

"If you think you can beat me in the race today, think again," Jason said as he stared at Dan with his beady little dark eyes. "If I were you, I would back out of the race."

"Get out of my way, Jason," Dan said, trying not to sound nervous. "You don't scare me! Now, get out of my way, so I can get to class." Jason looked stunned as Dan walked past him toward his class. Dan's heart was pounding in fear, but he felt proud as he slid into his desk. He was thankful that Jason sat on the other side of the classroom.

That afternoon the entire school went to

the Clover Country Track Meet. Foxy, Johnny and Holly picked the best bleacher seats that they could find. They were looking at the track field below, trying to find Dan.

"There he is!" Johnny shouted, pointing at the starting line. The Greenhouse Kids watched nervously as Dan warmed up for the race by shaking his hands and feet. The loudspeakers crackled, announcing that the runners should take their marks. They knelt down, ready to sprint. Speedy Seedy was in lane three and Dan was in lane four.

"Hey turtle, hope you choke on my dust," Speedy Seedy teased Dan in a sneering voice. Dan decided to ignore him and stared straight ahead, thinking about winning the race.

"On your marks, get set, GO!" Coach Stanton bellowed.

Everyone in the bleachers was jumping up and down, waving their school flags and cheering for their favourite runners. The runners got off to a fast start with Speedy Seedy in the lead, and Dan close behind. They had to complete one lap around

the track. The runners were neck and neck, and by the time they reached the half-way mark, Dan could see Speedy Seedy in front of him. It felt like the others were breathing down his neck. Dan tried to pick up his pace, running as fast as he could. The gap between Speedy Seedy and Dan was lessening. Dan was catching up to Speedy Seedy! The finish line was nearing and Dan heard his friends and classmates cheering him on. He also remembered Speedy Seedy calling him a turtle. This made him want to win even more! Suddenly, Dan felt he had trust and faith that he could win the race. "I am going to win this race," he said to himself. He saw Speedy Seedy out of the corner of his eye as he passed by him. He raised his arms and went through the finish line! Dan did it! He won the race! He slowed down, falling to the ground and panting for breath. Jason glared at him angrily and slithered away, defeated. Dan was glad to see him leave.

The Greenhouse Kids rushed out of the bleachers to pick him up and slap high fives.

They were so glad that he won! This was one of the happiest moments in Dan's life, and he didn't think he would ever forget winning the race, surrounded by the best friends in the world.

"We knew you could win!" Johnny said, slapping Dan on the back.

"Yes, I thought there was a good chance that you would win," Virginia Creeper piped up. Somehow she had suddenly appeared, and was gone again just as quickly.

"Geez!" Foxy said as she jumped in surprise. "How does she always creep up on us like that?"

"I don't know," said Holly, laughing. "At least she thought Dan could win! She can't be that bad!"

They were anxious to get to the greenhouse so that Dan could thank Lucinda the Ladybug for the magical carrots. "If it weren't for those magical carrots that Lucinda the Ladybug gave me, I might not have won the race," Dan said.

"Can we get Madison on the way?" Foxy asked. "It might be a good idea to have the

103

extra eyes and ears!" Foxy always felt much better having Madison with them.

The Greenhouse Kids rushed through the greenhouse door shouting that Dan had won the race. Even Madison was barking as if she was trying to shout the news!

"Lucinda, I could not have won the race without your magical carrots," Dan said. "How can I ever thank you enough?"

Lucinda the Ladybug asked The Greenhouse Kids to gather around her as she had something very important to tell them. They were surprised when she told them that Dan did not win the race because of her magical carrots.

Dan looked at Lucinda the Ladybug in shock! "Lucinda, what do you mean? I ate them every day just like you told me to."

"I know you did, Dan. But there were no magical powers in any of the carrot seeds that you planted, or in the carrots that I gave you. I know that you thought that the carrots had magical powers, but they did not. There was no magic in any of the seeds that I gave to Foxy,

Holly, and Johnny either. You won the race because you practised hard every day. You believed in yourself and you were willing to go the distance. You gained confidence."

"What does willing to go the distance mean?" Johnny asked.

"It means that you are willing to finish or complete something, even though it is very difficult or challenging," Lucinda the Ladybug replied. She also told them that Foxy's lemons, Holly's sunflowers and Johnny's pumpkins grew so well because they were nourished and cared for every day. "Do you remember when we were planting our seeds? I explained to you that you had to take care of your plants every day?"

"Yes," Holly replied. The others nodded their heads in agreement.

"Sometimes the same can be said for people," Lucinda the Ladybug explained. "There is a saying that people can be like well-watered gardens, blooming and doing well. And that is just what Dan did in the race. He worked hard, he had trust and faith in

himself, and it allowed him to do well! The only magic in the seeds was how quickly they would grow. The rest of the magic was inside all of you. It comes from your heart and all of your hard work. Each one of you is extra special, and you've made me very proud." she said. "Congratulations, Dan!" She then turned to them and said, "Keep up the good work!"

CHAPTER 17
THE TIN BOX

The Greenhouse Kids were bursting with pride as they left the greenhouse, heading toward the tombstones.

"I think we should go down the tunnel and get back inside that old mansion tonight," Dan said. "Whatever is going on, I think we'll find a clue inside the house!"

"Are you nuts?" Johnny asked.

"I think Dan is right," Holly added. "Tomorrow is the last day of school, so none of us have any homework to do."

"This time we'll bring an extra flashlight," Dan said. "I can get a hammer from my dad's tool shed to take down the board that is across the front door. My dad showed me how to use a hammer and some other tools when we built my go-cart. I'll bring a

screwdriver too, in case we need it to open something," Dan said.

"Okay," Johnny replied slowly, not sure if he really wanted to go. "Let's meet after supper at the bottom of the hill. My mom's working late tonight, so I won't be able to meet you until seven o'clock. Is that okay?"

They agreed to meet. At seven o'clock, with their tools in hand, they returned up the hill. Madison had to stay behind as it was after supper.

"Can't we do this during the day?" Foxy wanted to know. "I miss Madison."

"That sounds good to me!" Johnny cried out.

"We could go on Saturday, but I want to go tonight," Dan replied. "I can't wait to go back into the house and see what we can find!"

They went up the hill and waited behind the bushes while Dan went up ahead. Soon, they heard Dan whistle three times and they hurried up the hill. They walked toward the tombstones. The mansion was in darkness, and some of the vines were swinging in the

breeze, making strange whispering sounds. They crept up to the shed, entered, and quietly pulled open the trap door.

Dan went down the ladder first, followed by Holly, Johnny and Foxy. They held their breath as they inched their way through the dark tunnel, not making a sound. Dan held his finger to his lips as he placed his ear against the entrance door into the house. He didn't hear anything and waved at the others to come forward. The door opened without being pushed, but it made an awful creaking sound. They stopped and listened, barely breathing. It was quiet, so they went up the stairs and into the kitchen.

"Help me take this board off of the front door," Dan said as he crossed the living room floor with the hammer and flashlight. "It will be a lot easier to run out the front door, just in case we need to leave in a hurry." The board came off easily as Dan pulled the nails out with the hammer. They were happy to see the front door open and close.

"Why don't we split up?" Dan suggested.

"Foxy and I can look in the kitchen while Holly and Johnny check out the living room."

"What are we, like, looking for?" Johnny asked as he pulled a cobweb out of his purple hair.

"I'm not really sure," Dan replied as he chewed on his lip. "Look through drawers. Look for secret hiding places. Check behind the pictures on the wall, or under the furniture. Maybe there is another trap door in here. You never know what we'll find."

They began searching the rooms. Dan was walking across the kitchen when he noticed a floorboard that creaked louder than the others and it sounded hollow. "I think I've found something here!" Dan shouted out in excitement. Holly and Johnny rushed into the kitchen.

"Listen! There might be something underneath here. This board sounds funny," Dan said as he took out his screwdriver and began to lift the floorboard. Once he removed it, he peered down with his flashlight. "I was right! There's a tin box down here! Johnny,

help me move this other board so that I can grab the tin box!"

They were down on their hands and knees surrounding the hole in the floor. Dan reached down and pulled up a small silver-coloured tin box that had a tiny lock on it. "It's locked! It looks like we will have to wait to open it," he said.

"Let's leave and we can try to open it at Foxy's lemonade stand," Holly suggested. "This place gives me the creeps!"

They all agreed and had just stood up to leave when they heard footsteps coming from the tunnel! Someone was coming down the tunnel toward the house. Frightened, they quickly ran to the front door, opened it, and sped toward the tombstones. Dan tucked the tin box under his arm. "Johnny, can you keep up with us?" Dan asked.

"Yeah, I'm okay," Johnny said as he panted for air.

"Look!" Foxy said as she pointed toward the shed. "Someone put that ghost into the tree branches over there. They're trying to scare us

111

away! Whoever is in the house will see that we lifted the boards off of the kitchen floor. We didn't have time to put them back over the hole!"

"We took the board off the front door too!" Holly added. "We left that on the living room floor!"

"Let's get to Foxy's lemonade stand as quickly as we can," Dan replied. "I have a feeling there is a clue in this little tin box!"

Once they reached the lemonade stand safely, they breathed a sigh of relief. Dan began to hammer the tiny lock on the tin box. The lock finally broke and he slowly opened the box, not sure what he would find. The others watched, anxious to see what was inside.

"What if there's a treasure in here?" Foxy giggled.

Dan looked into the open box. "It's just a bunch of papers! At the top of the page it says "Morris, Smithson & Partners, Barristers Chambers." It says they're from somewhere in London, England."

"I think a barrister is like a lawyer," Holly

said.

Dan spread the papers out on the stand, and they began to read them. "Look!" Holly said. "It says that these are adoption papers! Marigold Ivy was adopted! I'll bet that's why that newspaper story about the English Ivys didn't say anything about Marigold! They must have adopted her sometime after that newspaper story was written."

"Here's the adoption date," Foxy exclaimed. "You're right, Holly! The adoption papers are dated at the end of July, 1982. I remember that newspaper story was dated at the beginning of July, 1982!"

"Foxy, your memory is totally amazing! I can't believe you remembered that," Holly replied.

"Wait! Look at this!" Dan said excitedly. "Marigold's last name was Creeper! Do you think she could be related to Virginia Creeper? Hey, check this out!" Dan lifted a delicate gold locket in the shape of a heart that was buried underneath the adoption papers. "Open it up!" he exclaimed, as he handed the locket to Holly.

113

She opened the gold locket, and on the inside there was a picture of a girl. "It must be Marigold Ivy, or Creeper, or whatever her last name is. She sort of looks like Virginia Creeper! They have the same brown eyes and wavy black hair. But Marigold doesn't have bright red lips or weird pointed ears like Virginia."

It was beginning to get dark, and time to go home. Dan placed the papers and the gold locket back into the tin box and closed the lid. "I think it's time we talked to Virginia."

"With the way she keeps creeping up on us, she'll probably find us before we find her!" Johnny said, laughing.

"Let's bring this tin box to Lucinda the Ladybug tomorrow," Dan said. We'll be getting out of school early and we can get to the greenhouse right away!"

Dan told them that he would keep the tin box safe at his house overnight. They all agreed that was a very good idea.

CHAPTER 18
WHAT GREENHOUSE?

The last day of school finally arrived. It was a sunny day, and once school ended, they walked to their secret clubhouse to show Lucinda the Ladybug the little tin box they had found. When they got to the top of the hill, they turned toward the cemetery.

Suddenly, Virginia Creeper and Speedy Seedy jumped out from behind bushes at the side of the road, scaring them half to death.

"Virginia Creeper! Jason Seedy! What are you two doing up here? Scaring us out of our wits!" Holly blurted out. She didn't get a chance to hear their answer, because Virginia and Jason quickly turned and began to run toward the cemetery. If they kept running into the backyard, they were sure to find the greenhouse!

"C'mon," Dan exclaimed. "We've got to follow them. They're headed right toward the greenhouse! They might find Lucinda the Ladybug!"

Dan held on tightly to the tin box as he chased after Virginia and Speedy Seedy, who were running into the backyard. It was too late. Speedy Seedy was too fast. He got to the greenhouse before the others could catch up to him. Virginia and Dan arrived at the same time, to find Speedy Seedy standing directly in front of the greenhouse! Holly and Foxy caught up to them and heard Dan talking to him. Johnny was still running toward them.

"So, I see you have found our greenhouse," Dan said, as he panted for air. Johnny arrived, and all of them looked at Speedy Seedy, waiting for him to say something. They were very upset that he had found their greenhouse.

"You guys are totally nuts! What greenhouse? What are you talking about? There's nothing here! All I see are big bushes and a bunch of weeds."

They looked at Virginia, who raised her dark eyebrows at Jason. "Jason, are you telling me that you don't see a greenhouse?" Virginia asked.

"That's right," he replied. "And I made a big mistake coming here to help you. When you asked me to help you search the mansion, I only said I would because I wanted to scare them." He glared at Dan, still angry that he had been beaten in the race. Virginia didn't say anything as Speedy Seedy turned around and ran back toward the road. They were happy to see him go.

Virginia could see the greenhouse, but Speedy Seedy could not. This puzzled The Greenhouse Kids. Holly looked at Virginia and said, "You can see the greenhouse, can't you?"

"Yes, I can. I never knew it was here, though. This is the first time that I have been back here. Let's go inside. Have you been inside the greenhouse yet?"

Holly told her that they had been inside the greenhouse many times. She was not ready to tell her about Lucinda the Ladybug.

117

"Besides, maybe Virginia won't be able to see Lucinda the Ladybug, just like Speedy Seedy couldn't see the greenhouse," she thought to herself.

Before they knew it, Virginia walked through the greenhouse door, and she was shocked to see Lucinda the Ladybug zooming around the greenhouse, her red cape flapping in the air, as she left a dazzling trail of colourful glitter. She landed on a large plant leaf in front of Virginia and grew to the size of a basketball.

"Hello, Virginia Creeper," Lucinda the Ladybug said in a soothing voice.

"So, Virginia *can* see Lucinda the Ladybug," Holly said to herself.

"What's going on?" Virginia asked as she jumped back in surprise.

"Please sit down, Virginia," Lucinda the Ladybug replied. "This is going to be a very long story!"

118

CHAPTER 19
JEEPERS CREEPERS

Lucinda the Ladybug told Virginia how Dan had found the greenhouse. She explained that each one of them was extra special because both their first and last names were named after flowers and plants.

"And, most importantly, they also share a likeness with the flowers and plants that they were named after," she added. "That is why you can also see me and the greenhouse."

Suddenly, she whirled around the greenhouse, her red cape flapping behind her. Her trail of glitter spelled out *Virginia Creeper* in green and red sparkling letters.

Lucinda the Ladybug flew back on the plant leaf in front of Virginia, who was standing with her bright red mouth gaping open in awe. "Gather around, everyone.

119

Virginia is also one of the extra special people in the world because she was named after a fast-growing vine called Virginia creeper. The vine attaches to anything that it creeps along. It is often found growing on houses and fences."

"She *is* just like a vine! She has been creeping up on us all year!" Johnny said.

"And," Lucinda the Ladybug added, "the vine Virginia creeper turns bright red in autumn. That is why Virginia Creeper has such bright red lips! And her little pointed ears are shaped just like the leaf on the vine. Most important, I think you will learn that once you get to know Virginia, just like the vine, she will begin to grow on you!" Lucinda the Ladybug explained. "If you think you don't like someone, all you need to do is get to know them better. Chances are you will find that you have more in common with them than you thought."

They all stared at Virginia Creeper's bright red lips and small pointy ears. Holly did not know it yet, but she would find Lucinda

VIRGINIA CREEPER

the Ladybug's words to be very true.

"Now you can understand why Jason Seedy could not see the greenhouse. Nor will he ever be able to see me," Lucinda the Ladybug explained. "He does not share his full

name with a flower or a plant!"

"So we are extra special, and Jason is not!" Foxy exclaimed.

Dan didn't say anything, but he was secretly glad that there were only a few extra special people who would ever be able to see the greenhouse or Lucinda the Ladybug. And he was lucky enough to be one of them!

"We have some questions for Virginia," Holly said. She told Virginia about the tin box that they found with the adoption papers. Holly asked Virginia if she knew anything about it.

"Well, yes. Marigold Ivy was related to me. She was my cousin."

"We thought you looked a bit alike!" Foxy exclaimed.

"I am sorry that I never met her. Something happened to my aunt and uncle and they couldn't take care of Marigold. The English Ivys were my grandparents, and they adopted her when she was about two years old. My grandparents also died when I was very little. I did meet them a few times, but I

don't remember them."

"I met you in the mall with your mother, and she spoke with an accent," Holly said. "Was she from England too?"

"Yes," Virginia replied. "My mother moved here from England. Most of my relatives still live in England. Marigold's last name was Creeper, just like mine. When my grandparents adopted Marigold, her last name was changed to Ivy. Even though Marigold was older than me, it would have been fun to know her. Ever since I found out about her I have been wearing black, because that is what people do when they are sad at a funeral."

"So that is why you are always wearing black. Virginia, we're sorry," Johnny said.

Foxy, Dan and Holly told Virginia how sorry they were.

"Virginia, you have to promise not to tell anyone about the greenhouse or Lucinda the Ladybug," Holly said. "Do you think you can keep this a secret?"

"Yes, and I don't want any of you to say anything about Marigold or the English Ivys.

I would like to keep that a secret too," she replied. "I told Speedy Seedy that I found the tunnel at the house. I asked him if he would help me search the house. I never told him what I was looking for, or anything about Marigold or the English Ivys.

"There is something else I need to tell you," Virginia confessed. "I asked Speedy Seedy if he would help me because his father is the Mayor. I thought his father could help me look up some information at the Town Hall. I didn't know that the only reason Speedy Seedy agreed to help me was so that he could scare all of you."

"It doesn't surprise us. That bully has been picking on us all year. I think this belongs to you," Dan said as he handed Virginia the tin box. Virginia took the tin box and opened it. She read the adoption papers and lifted the delicate gold heart-shaped locket.

"Thank you. I thought I might find something like this in the house. I can also explain the awful crashing sound that you heard while you were in the house. We were upstairs, looking out the window, and we

saw you go into the shed. We waited to see if you found the tunnel. We knew that you did when we heard you come up into the kitchen. It was Jason's idea to try to scare you away. He knocked a stack of books off a table. He made that little ghost that you found outside too."

"Well, we weren't that scared," Johnny fibbed. "Speedy Seedy doesn't scare us!"

"I knew you found something when I saw the hole in the kitchen floor," Virginia told them.

"Virginia, would you like me to put this locket on you?" Holly asked.

"Thanks, Holly. That would be awesome!" Virginia replied as she handed Holly the locket. Holly clasped it around Virginia's neck. "I think I should give up wearing black all the time. Do you think you could come to the mall with me and help me shop? You have the coolest clothes!"

"Sure, I would like to help you. Let me know when you want to go," Holly answered. "I think Lucinda the Ladybug is right. You're

starting to grow on me already!"

"It looks like this is going to be a great summer!" Dan exclaimed. "I have a feeling Speedy Seedy won't be bothering us any more."

"I am glad everything has worked out so perfectly," Lucinda the Ladybug told them. "I am very proud of all of you."

"Lucinda, do you think that I could grow some seeds too?" Virginia asked.

"Funny you should ask," Lucinda the Ladybug replied. "I think you will be quite excited to learn about the new seeds that I have for all of you to grow." She held out many packets of seeds for them to see. But the packets were completely blank! They did not know what the seeds were! Everyone held out their hands in excitement, their hearts thumping wildly.

"Sorry, but you can't have these seed packets yet. When you're ready to plant them, I will let you know," Lucinda the Ladybug told them.

"When will that be?" Foxy asked.

"Don't worry! I will let you know. For now

126

it's a secret. I do have a clue for you, though. The clue is that you will need to meet someone new at school first," Lucinda the Ladybug replied.

"Who do we need to meet first?" Holly asked as she furrowed her eyebrows.

"Once you answer that riddle, then we can talk about planting these special seeds," Lucinda the Ladybug replied. "You'll find out soon enough. Now, go out and enjoy your summer vacation!"

The Greenhouse Kids looked at each other, wondering what Lucinda the Ladybug meant by her words. They left the greenhouse, talking excitedly.

Virginia and Holly became especially close friends that summer. Holly had a shopping partner every Saturday and everyone welcomed Virginia Creeper as the newest member of The Greenhouse Kids. They all agreed that Lucinda the Ladybug was right! Virginia Creeper was definitely growing on all of them!

The End

127

About the Author

 Shelley Awad was born in Windsor, Ontario in 1958 and currently lives nearby in Tecumseh with her husband, Mitch. She has one son, Aaron, who is completing his PhD in chemistry at the University of Windsor.

She received her Journalism Diploma from St. Clair College in Windsor. In 1999, Shelley opened her own greenhouse business, Backyard Greenhouses, specializing in residential and commercial greenhouses that she continues to sell across North America.